Special People, Special Ways

Future Horizons, Inc. • Arlington, Texas

Published by
Future Horizons, Inc.
721 W. Abram Street
Arlington, TX 76013
www.FutureHorizons-autism.com

Copyright 2000 by Future Horizons, Inc. 1-800-489-0727
Artwork Copyright by Sheila Bailey
Text Copyright by Arlene Maguire
All rights reserved.

Design: BOARDWALK
Edited by Christina D. Carpenter

Publisher's Cataloging-in-Publication
Maguire, Arlene H., 1940-
        Special People, Special Ways/by Arlene Maguire;
illustrated by Sheila Lucas Bailey. -- 1st ed.
        p. cm.
        SUMMARY: A poem about the ways in which people with
many differences in physical and mental ability, even as they share
the same human needs for love and understanding.
        Preassigned LCCN: 98-87351
        ISBN: 1-885477-65-1
        1. Handicapped--Juvenile poetry. 2. Toleration--Juvenile poetry.
        I. Lucas, Sheila, ill. II. Title
HV1568.M34 1999   362.4
                         QBI98-1232

DEDICATED TO

The Binetskys
Lisa, Beth, Harriet and Bebe

Tria Psaropulos

Jim Bobryk

Sarah and Issac Bonyor

Though people look different
We share hopes and fears,
Giggles and grumbles,
Our dreams and our tears.

Not everyone born
Is athletic or smart;
We each have a choice
To give from our heart.

All people shine
As jewels in a chest.
Born with our gifts
Each person is blessed.

Some see with a touch
Or shape fingers to talk.
Others sit silent
And many can't walk.

Some pilot a wheelchair,
Guide a walker or cane.
And lots of good people
Struggle with pain.

Creams flow from small tubes
To soothe where it aches,
And many seek cures
For jitters and shakes.

Hands at a keyboard
Make mum voices heard,
Since lips of some people
Form barely a word.

Sometimes it's hard
To get through the day.
But we do what we can
In our very own way.

There are those who are fed
Or helped to get dressed.
But everyone's proud,
Having given their best.

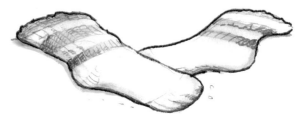

Thousands wear glasses
Or use gadgets to hear.

Fine mists and face masks
Help some to breathe air.

Animals serve
Like dogs, as a guide.
And monkeys well trained
To help along side.

Plenty learn slowly
When trying to read;
But everyone's special
At fast or slow speed.

We help when we can
Should someone need aid;
Giving and taking
Bring wonder in trade.

Share a joke or a dream.
Make someone feel good.
We need laughter, hugs,
And to be understood.

Be thoughtful to all
As you would a good friend,
Since the hurts that we feel
Are not easy to mend.

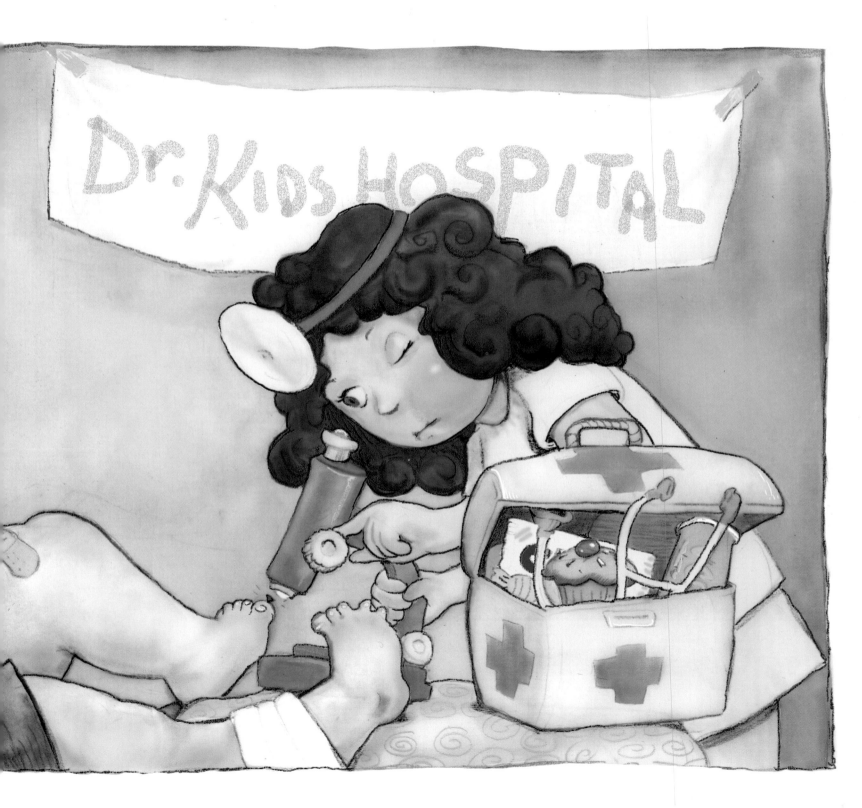

Though we seem different
Inside we're the same.
Our hearts are for caring
No matter our name.